CANNONBALL
SIMP

Written and Illustrated
(by)
JOHN BURNINGHAM

JONATHAN CAPE 30 BEDFORD SQUARE LONDON

for Acton

By the same author:

BORKA (Winner of the Kate Greenaway Award in 1964)

TRUBLOFF

ABC

HUMBERT

HARQUIN

SEASONS

MR GUMPY'S OUTING (Winner of the Kate Greenaway Award in 1971)

AROUND THE WORLD IN EIGHTY DAYS

MR GUMPY'S MOTOR CAR

And the John Burningham Wall Friezes:

BIRDLAND

LIONLAND

STORYLAND

JUNGLELAND

WONDERLAND

AROUND THE WORLD

First published 1966
Reprinted 1970, 1973, 1976
© 1966 by John Burningham

Jonathan Cape Ltd, 30 Bedford Square, London WCI

ISBN 0 224 61123 2

Printed and bound in Great Britain by Morrison & Gibb Ltd, London and Edinburgh

Simp was what most people would call an ugly little dog. She was fat and small, and had only a stump for a tail. Her owner had found homes for her brothers and sisters but could not persuade anybody to take Simp. So, in order to get rid of her, he decided to leave her somewhere, hoping that somebody would find her and take her in.

One evening he took Simp outside the town
and just dumped her near a rubbish pit.

Poor little Simp watched the van disappearing
into the distance. She could not understand
why she had been left all alone. She did not
know what to do. Then darkness fell. By the light
of the moon she explored the rubbish pit and
found an old armchair to spend the night in.
Rats came out and looked curiously at her.
When Simp said how hungry she was, one of
them gave her a piece of bread. "But you'll have
to go in the morning," he said. "It's hard enough
for us rats to live. There wouldn't be enough
food for you as well."

When it was light the next morning, Simp left
the rubbish pit and wandered off in the direction
of the town. She tried to make friends with
people who were going to work, but nobody
seemed to care about her. She spent a long time
searching for something to eat but she could
not find anything.

Then she came
across some dustbins.
She started looking
through them for food
and did not notice
the cats who were
angrily watching her.

"That's my dustbin," hissed one of the cats as he pounced. Simp ran for her life with the cat just behind her. She was running so fast that she did not look where she was going.

"Got you," said the dog-catcher. Two large hands grabbed Simp and she was put in the back of the van with the other strays which the dog-catcher had collected. Almost all the other dogs in the van had homes. "We often get picked up," they said. "But what will become of you with no home to go to? And you don't even have a collar."

Simp became more and more worried as she talked to the other dogs. "Who can tell what may happen to you now?" one said. "You're not very pretty, are you?—and you're fat and muddy," said another. "I doubt if anybody will want to give you a home," said a third.

The van pulled into the yard of the dog pound. The doors were opened and the dogs driven towards the kennels. When the dog-catcher was looking the other way Simp saw her chance. She jumped up on some boxes and was away over the wall.

Simp kept running and running until she was well out of town. Then, because she was still frightened, she crept into some thick bushes to hide. By the time it was dark she had become very hungry and set off again down the road.

Then, in the distance, Simp saw lights. They were the lights of a circus.

She went towards them, hoping she might find
someone there who would give her some food.

Perhaps after that she could curl up under a
caravan where it would be a little warmer.

She crept up to a caravan, climbed on a box
and looked through the window. Inside was a
clown who was very surprised to see a little dog
peering at him. He opened the door and
beckoned to Simp. "You look very tired and
hungry," said the clown, and he gave Simp a
large meal which she gobbled up. It was warm
and comfortable in the caravan and the clown
let Simp lie on his bed. She was soon fast asleep.

The next morning the clown showed Simp
round the circus. There were many tents,
caravans and animals. Simp met a young
elephant and a lion.

Everybody seemed happy and friendly, but the clown was worried. People did not like his act any more.

The clown told Simp exactly what he did. He showed her the cannon which fired a rubber ball through a paper hoop. Just then the ringmaster came up. "Unless you improve your act by tonight, you'll have to go," he said to the clown.

Simp had an idea. "That rubber ball is exactly the same size as me when I am curled up," she thought. "I just have time to work out a plan before the show starts."

The evening performance had begun. Just before the clown's act, Simp climbed into the cannon while nobody was looking. The man who was to fire the cannon peered inside and, seeing Simp curled up, thought she was the ball. Simp's heart was beating fast as she waited for the exciting moment to arrive.

The circus managers had a look of boredom on their faces as they watched the clown. "He'll really have to go," they said.

There was a rolling of drums and...

WHOOSH! Through the air flew Simp, straight for the paper hoop. Right through the hoop she went.

The crowds roared with delight when they saw that the 'cannon ball' was a little black dog. The clown was so surprised to see Simp that he almost dropped the hoop.

Simp landed on a drum and stood there proudly while the audience cheered and cheered. She had really quite enjoyed being fired from the cannon. Then the clown and Simp were put on a horse and they went round and round the ring. Everybody was still wildly clapping and cheering.

After the show, the ringmaster gave a party for Simp and the clown. He invited the little elephant, the lion and a monkey Simp had met, and they all ate until they were quite full up. The ringmaster told the clown and Simp that their act was the best the circus had ever had.

And so Simp lived happily with the clown and travelled round the countryside with the circus. The act became famous and people came especially to see the little dog fired from a cannon.

And that is how she came to be called Cannonball Simp.

THE END